Gilles

Hang on, Mooch

Illustrations by
Pierre-André Derome

Translated by
Sarah Cummins

Formac Publishing Limited
Halifax, Nova Scotia
1992

Originally published as Sauvez ma Babouche

Copyright © 1989 la courte échelle

Translation copyright © 1992 by Formac Publishing Limited

Canadian Cataloguing in Publication Data

Gauthier, Gilles, 1943-

[Sauvez ma Babouche. English]

Hang on, Mooch

(First novel series)

Translation of: Sauvez ma Babouche.

ISBN 0-88780-204-4 (pbk.)
ISBN 0-88780-205-2 (bound)

I. Derome, Pierre-André, 1952- II Title. III Title: Sauvez ma Babouche. English. IV Series.

PS8563.A858S2913 1992 jC843' .54 C92-098551-3
PZ7.G38Ha 1992

Formac Publishing Limited
5502 Atlantic Street
Halifax, N.S. B3H 1G4

Printed and bound in Canada.

Table of contents

1
Here a dog, there a dog.

"Hello, Gary? This is Carl. You've got to come over right away."

"I can't. I have to rake the lawn before winter comes."

"Forget about winter and just come over. Mooch has disappeared again."

"Not again!"

"Hurry! My mum will be home from work in exactly forty-five minutes."

"Do you know which way Mooch went?"

"No, all I know is that she might be miles away by now.

That dumb old Mooch! So hang up and get over here quick!"

Things have been going from bad to worse.

The problem is Mooch. I think she is losing her memory. She goes away and then she forgets to come back.

In the last two weeks she has gone missing four times and Gary and I have had to search for her. She thinks it's fun to get lost.

It wasn't so bad the first time. She was just next door at the Taylors' house. She was gnawing on an old chicken carcass that Smoky the cat had hidden away for a rainy day.

The second time she was at the outdoor track. Miss Mooch was out jogging with the crowd.

Last Sunday we found her down by the river. She was wallowing in a little mudhole, pretending to be a hippopotamus.

And the day before yesterday, we discovered her way back in the woods behind the house. She was so exhausted from chasing squirrels that she fell flat on her face every few steps on the way home.

I haven't mentioned any of this

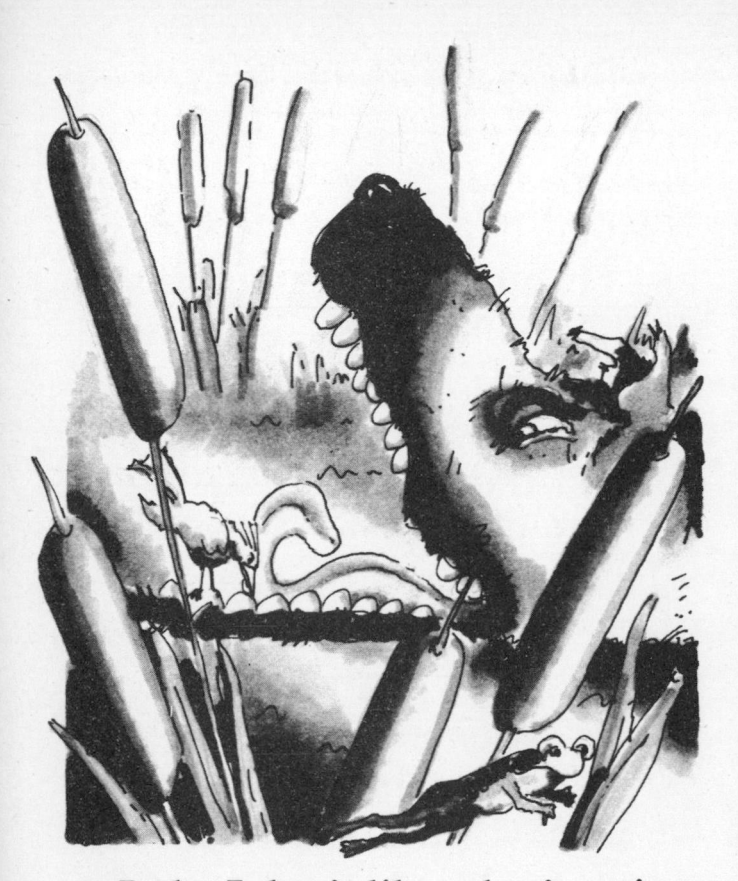

to Judy. I don't like what's going on. I'm worried about Mooch.

I would never have been able to find her on my own those four times. Fortunately, Gary is a real detective. It's as if he has ESP.

Actually, what he really does have is experience. Last year he spent more time roaming around outside than he did in school. He has tried every one of the secret hiding places in the neighbourhood.

The trouble with Mooch is she doesn't decide to hide in a particular place. She just keeps going and then—surprise! It's like she's landed on a different planet. She has no idea where she is. Even when she's only a block or two away from home.

2
Gary, before and after

Gary used to be my worst enemy. Now he's my best friend. I couldn't believe it at first. I didn't trust him one inch, not after all he had done to me.

I was always afraid he'd sneak up behind me, when I was least expecting it, and bonk me on the head. But he never did.

Ever since his dad came to live with him, Gary has been a new person.

I think he started getting interested in me when he found out my dad was dead. I had talked about that when our teacher asked us to present our family to the class.

Gary came up to me at recess and said that he would like to meet Mooch.

At first I thought he was making fun of me, like before. But he swore he wasn't and asked again to meet Mooch.

When we got home, I introduced him to Mooch and showed him my slides. He saw how Dad had given me Mooch when I was little.

Gary told me that he had always wanted a dog just like Mooch, especially when he was living with his aunt, before his dad came back.

At the exact moment Gary said that, a very strange thing happened.

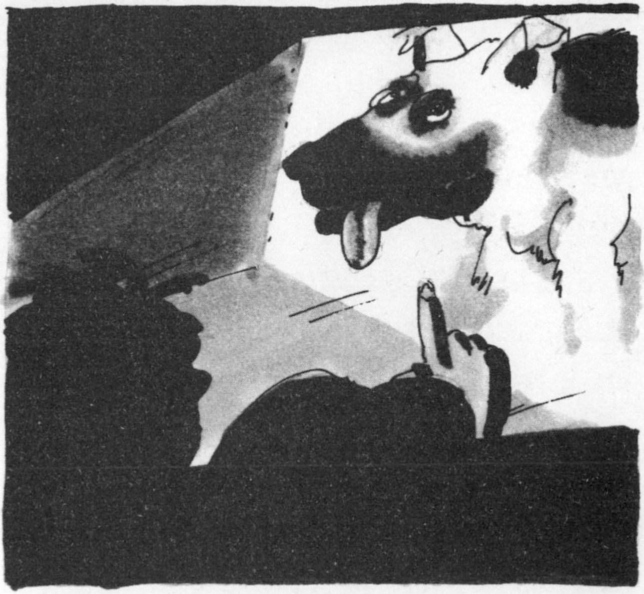

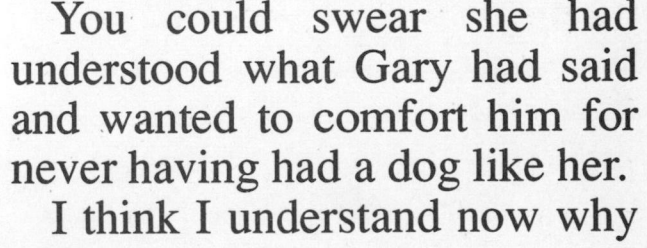

Mooch, who had just set eyes on Gary for the first time in her life, got up and quietly went over to lie down next to him. Just like that, without being called.

You could swear she had understood what Gary had said and wanted to comfort him for never having had a dog like her.

I think I understand now why

Gary used to act the way he did. He was jealous because I had a friend like Mooch at home, and so he tried to get back at me in school.

But that's all over now. Gary has told me he's sorry for what he did.

I could tell it was true, just by listening to him and seeing how he acts with Mooch.

He looks after her as if she were a tiny baby. And Mooch plays right up to him. She whimpers and whines all the time so he'll pet her.

And now the three of us are almost always together—Gary, Mooch, and me. The Three Musketeers!

One of us, however, is a four-legged musketeer who thinks she's a hippopotamus!

3
These doggone dog-catchers

"We've been through the whole neighbourhood three times. I've run out of hiding places to look in."

"Think, Gary, think! Use your ESP. You've always found her before. You can't let her down now."

"I'm not letting her down. You are! Your mum must be back by now. If you tell her, she could help us."

"What am I supposed to tell her?"

"The truth, that's all. Just tell her what's happened."

"Then she'll decide that Mooch is over the hill, and she'll have her put down!"

"No, she won't! She'll help us find her, that's all. If you keep on like this, no one will have to decide anything anyway."

"What do you mean?"

"The dog-catchers will decide what to do with her."

The dog-catchers! I'd rather not even think of it. What would they do with an old dog like Mooch?

I can just imagine.

They'll try to talk to her but she won't understand a word. They'll try to put her in a cage and she'll fight like crazy. She won't know where she is because she can't see anything.

Once she's locked up, she'll

howl like a prisoner on Death Row.

She'll be afraid. They'll tell her to be quiet.

She won't be quiet. Then they'll...they'll...

For the people at the pound, she's just an old lost dog.

But for me, she's Mooch. My Mooch.

4
Wanted: Mooch

Judy has phoned the pound to see if they have anything resembling our dog locked up in their cages. She left our number and they're supposed to call back.

She had to describe Mooch to them. It's just as well Mooch didn't hear that part. She would have been shattered.

She still thinks she's as young as ever. It would have been a rude awakening for her. Judy all but told them that Mooch has to walk with a cane!

"A sort of German Shepherd, fairly old, with grey, matted fur, droopy ears, a ragged tail..."

She might just as well have called Mooch a prehistoric beast! Really, she shouldn't exaggerate. Mooch is old, but she's no antique.

I'm not at all sure anyone would recognize Mooch from Judy's description, even if she were standing right in front of them.

Mooch is Mooch, that's all there is to it.

She isn't really like other dogs, that's true.

She is a bit short for a German Shepherd, that's true.

She does look a bit like a giant hairy caterpillar when she hasn't been brushed. And even when she has. But she's not the Abominable Snowdog!

Mooch is extremely sensitive. If she is indeed locked up in a dark little cage somewhere right now, she must be scared out of her mind.

Despite appearances, she is a very intelligent dog. And she would never hurt a fly. Not even the peskiest fly.

The telephone is ringing. Judy picks it up. She listens, but

doesn't say anything.

Then she says, "Yes…yes."

Then, "No."

Then, "Yes, that's all right. We'll be there in about half an hour."

Judy hangs up. She's crying. Oh no, it's all over!

Judy's laughing. She's crying for joy. Mooch is still alive!

5
Behind bars

Gary's dad drove us to the pound. Gary phoned him from our house.

Gary's dad is pretty nice, even if he doesn't talk much. He seems nervous.

When Gary introduced him to Judy, he looked embarrassed, and he didn't know what to say. He just nodded his head.

Now Judy is talking to a man at the pound. Wait! I think I hear a dog barking! But that's not Mooch's bark.

Mooch's bark has been all raspy lately. She barks like a dog that is a heavy smoker. Maybe she's been smoking in secret!

The man asks us to come with him. The barks are getting closer, but I still don't hear Mooch's voice.

I hope they didn't make a mistake. The way Judy described her, it wouldn't surprise me if they did.

We come to the cages. All the dogs are whining and complaining. I can't wait to find Mooch.

You wouldn't believe how many dogs there are in the pound. It's like a zoo. There are all kinds of them.

That's a poodle. She's funny-looking.

That one is a dachshund. It looks like its legs forgot to grow.

And the black one is a pit bull.

The newspapers are full of stories about pit bulls. It has a square head almost as big as its body. Compared to a pit bull, Mooch looks like Miss Universe.

Yikes! What is that huge dog? Gary's dad says it's a Great Dane. It's bigger than Gary and me together laid end to end.

With its tail hitting everything,

everywhere, it's like a walking one-dog drum solo.

And who is that I see, huddled back in the corner against the wall?

Maybe it's not her. But yes, it is, it's her.

It's Mooch!

She has just recognized us. She gets up like a cyclone and tries to break through the bars of her cage.

"Stop, Mooch. You'll hurt yourself. Wait, wait. The man will open the cage for you."

Mooch is howling her head off and not listening to a word I say.

"Please hurry, sir. My dog wants out."

The guy from the pound takes his own sweet time. He's

shuffling papers around. Gary's dad gets impatient and decides he is going to open the cage himself.

Mooch leaps up on me, yapping, crying, whimpering.

"Yes, Mooch, it's me."

No, you big silly, don't worry about it. It was my fault. I forgot to put your collar on.

Of course, I understand what you're saying, Mooch. I can't wait to get out of here either.

6
Heavy hearts

Mooch was excited all the way home. She stretched out across my lap, breathing about five hundred times a minute.

Her heart was beating so loud I could feel it in my chest. I thought it was my own heart.

When we got home, Mooch ran to the door and barked and howled until Judy opened it.

She shot inside like a rocket and ran upstairs and hid under my bed.

When I crawled closer to pet her, it suddenly seemed to me that she had aged by at least ten

years. She was shaking.

Gary's dad stayed a little while longer, talking with Judy in a low voice. When it was time to go, he came into the room to get Gary.

I could tell he wanted to say something to me, but he had a lump in his throat. Finally he left without saying anything.

Judy was trying to hold back her tears too.

I lay down on the floor next to Mooch and talked to her for a long time. She was still scared. Her eyes were big and round.

I told her there was no need to worry any more. The terrible nightmare was over.

I told her how Gary had searched for her everywhere. I told her how Judy had called the pound. I told her how Gary's dad

had freed her from her cage.

And I talked about Dad.

I told her Dad would have asked her to get back on her feet as soon as possible so she could keep on looking after Mum and me.

Later, Judy told me I fell asleep on the rug about midnight. I was drained, just like Mooch. I had run out of words.

7
Gary's secret

Gary came over to our house to see how Mooch was doing. He lay down beside her and stroked her over and over, without saying anything.

Mooch thought this was a fine time to wash Gary's hand and arm with her long wet tongue.

Then Gary started talking. He spoke quietly for a long time, in fits and starts.

He said that he used to tell lies all the time at school. His dad had never taken a trip around the world. The whole time he had been away, four years, he was in prison, a sort of pound for humans.

Every second for four years, Gary hid what he was thinking from everyone. For four years, he acted tough at school, in case anyone should find out. He could only start living without having to lie when his dad came back to him.

Listening to Gary made me think of Mooch in the pound, all alone behind steel bars. And I thought of how Gary's dad had opened the door to free her.

Gary went on. He said he was telling me his secret because I was his only true friend. That gave me a nice, warm feeling inside, which reminded me of something long ago.

I thought and thought, but I

couldn't put my finger on what the feeling reminded me of.

Gary told me his dad had a lot of trouble finding a job when he got out of jail. But things are starting to work out.

He said that, after seeing Mooch, his dad had promised to

get Gary a puppy for his birthday, if all goes well.

I looked at my old dog who had dropped off to sleep, leaning against Gary's arm. And then in a flash I knew where that feeling of warmth a long time ago had come from.

I remembered Dad putting a tiny black ball of fur into my crib with me. Mooch was so soft, so warm.

Dad had given me a friend.

8
Mooch will always
come back

When I woke up this morning and looked down at the foot of my bed, I got a terrible shock. For a second, I thought that Mooch had stopped breathing.

Mooch was dead.

But she wasn't really. A few seconds later I could see that her chest was rising and falling gently, just as usual.

Still, from that moment on, I knew that Mooch wouldn't be with us too much longer.

I knew that Judy and the vet were right. You might be able to rescue a dog from the pound, but you can't save a dog from getting old and dying.

I burst into tears.

Judy came running and she took me in her arms.

"What's wrong, Carl? Why are you crying?"

I gulped out, between sobs, "Because…Mooch…is going to die…soon!"

Judy didn't say anything for a long time. She held me close and softly sang a little lullaby she used to sing to put me to sleep.

Then she told me a story, like she used to.

"Once upon a time there was a boy. He was nine years old and he had a dog with an extra-ordinary ability. This dog would always, always come back, no

matter what.

"Very few people knew that this ability even existed. Most people thought that the dog would disappear some day, forever, without a trace.

"But that boy and everyone else who loved this dog knew that this was not true. They knew that any place, any time, they had only to close their eyes, and they could call the dog back. Then they could see her and talk to her,

just like before. Because that old dog will live forever in the hearts of all those who loved her."

When Judy had finished, Mooch opened her eyes and looked at us. I could swear she was smiling.

9
It's not over yet

Isn't that just like Mooch! Just when everyone thinks she's on her death-bed, she springs back.

I haven't seen her looking so well for a long time. You wouldn't recognize her. She is in her second childhood.

First she unearthed an old chewed-up rubber ball that was lost about ten years ago. She started tossing it in the air and yapping, like she used to do with Dad.

When Mooch was a baby, she liked to play baseball.

Now Mooch wants to play

hide-and-seek. She insists I hide in the bathroom, like I used to. Then she comes in and finds me, and I have to pretend to be surprised.

Sometimes it takes her twenty minutes to find me. It makes me wonder whether she is seeking or hiding.

Once, I had enough time to count to two thousand and two before she came. I was beginning to get a bit bored. But not Mooch! She is having the time of her life.

After baseball and hide-and-seek, we have to go for a walk. Not just a stroll, mind you. This is power-walking. A real marathon!

Mooch pulls so hard on the leash that it feels as if my arms will come out of their sockets.

She looks as if she's saying, "And you thought I was on my last legs, eh Carl? Well, I've got news for you. You'll soon see that Mooch has got quite a long way to go yet."

Gary cannot figure out what's going on. He thinks it must be

part of her memory loss, and now she can't remember that she's old. He says I had better get her to take it easy.

I let him talk, but I know that he's wrong. I know Mooch pretty well by now.

Mooch is a very proud dog. She doesn't want us to think she's got one foot in the grave. She's decided to make us eat our words.

She's not about to die today, or tomorrow, or even the day after tomorrow. No way!

When she's good and ready, then she'll die, and not a minute sooner.

Mooch will decide when. Not me, not the vet, not Judy, and not Gary.

Looking at her now, I think

she's got her second wind. And she's decided to live to the fullest in the time remaining.

I agree with her one hundred per cent!

Death will just have to wait. And if Death doesn't like it, Death can go away and forget about Mooch.

That would be just fine with everyone.

The First Novel series

If you enjoyed this book, you'll enjoy these other First Novels — available now at your local bookstore!

Arthur's Dad
by Ginette Anfousse

Arthur's dad is about to give up because he can't find a babysitter for Arthur. He has already had twenty-three! But now perhaps Arthur has met his match ...

That's Enough, Maddie
by Louise Leblanc

Maddie has quite a problem. Her whole family is getting on her nerves. So she decides to run away from home ... but what do you do when supper time rolls around?

Maddie in Goal
by Louise Leblanc

Maddie dreams of being a hockey goalie, so she tries to convince the all-boys team to let her play. When it's time for the big game, she decides to make sure that she'll be able to play...

The Swank Prank
by Bertrand Gauthier

Hank and Frank Swank are twins. Trying to be the smartest kids in school takes a lot of work. Can they do it?

Swank Talk
by Bertrand Gauthier

The Swank twins have found a way to confuse everyone: no one can understand what they're saying! It takes another set of twins to put them back in touch with the world.

Mooch and Me
by Gilles Gauthier

Carl and his best friend Mooch are nine. But, Mooch is a dog and that makes him 63! He is old, deaf and almost blind, and he gets Carl into lots of trouble. But Carl thinks he's the best dog that ever lived!

The Loonies Arrive
by Christiane Duchesne

One night Christopher finds some little people under his pillow — no more than three centimetres tall! It's not easy learning how to look after a collection of little people who make their home in your room ...